MY TWO LOST ANGELS

by Brien Lawrence

DORRANCE PUBLISHING CO
EST. 1920
PITTSBURGH, PENNSYLVANIA 15238

Dorrance Publishing Co
585 Alpha Drive
Suite 103
Pittsburgh, PA 15238
Visit our website at *www.dorrancebookstore.com*

ISBN: 979-8-8852-7104-2
eISBN: 979-8-8852-7831-7

To Donna, Shannon, Jamie, and Ricky.
You all know why.

To whom it might concern,

Thank you for being curious enough to pick up my story and interested enough to want to know more about me. I can not say what moves anyone to begin writing. I can only say that for me, I felt a need to explain myself and my actions to… no one really. The words just kept coming until they didn't. It is my sincerest wish that you enjoy the read and feel the emotional eddies that maturity brings.

CATALYST

When I was a young man navigating my way through high school, I was infatuated not only with girls but with a Doberman Pinscher that belonged to my surf bud. My name is Keith, and my friend Kurt found the pup somewhere and spent a year totally focused on the dog rather than the surf. The dog's name was Thor. I was so impressed with Thor's discipline, focus, and ferocious presence, that I wanted to emulate my friend/dog's relationship and find a companion of my own. I gave this no short order of thought. I wanted my dog to be as mighty as Thor. I wanted my dog to be trained and disciplined just like Thor. I decided I would choose a Pinscher just like Thor, and I would name him Tybalt to assure his antagonistic presence (Romeo & Juliette). I wanted the relationship with my dog to be just as I had observed the one of my friend Kurt and his companion Thor. As it seems to happen in my life, God granted my prayers with a twist, Bebo. Bebo would teach me things often spoken to me by my parents and friends, acknowledged and understood, but never felt.

THE EARLY YEARS

I came through high school breaking my foot at pre-season football practice in my freshman year, out for the season. I swear, it must have been the same hole in the practice field and I suffered an ankle injury in my sophomore year, again out for the season. While I was recovering from my injuries these two years, it was the season when the ocean sends its winter tide to the beach. I became fanatically challenged with the call, and very literally applied myself sunup to sundown, to learn how to surf well. I developed a relationship with my new teammates: the dolphins, coral reefs, sharks, barracudas, and powerful swells. Like in organized sports, we had unspoken signals to let each other know where we stood, and what direction to take. If we disobeyed these signals, one or both of us got hurt. I was entirely comfortable with this relationship and embraced the countless hours of solitude and harmony. I found myself dedicated to all seasons of this challenge.

It was during this time that I found my companion. He was a she, and the intimidating, pedigreed Doberman was determined by the vet to be a Dobi-Lab-mix. She was not to become a 105-pound monster like Thor, but a medium-sized forty-five-pound hot rod. I was therefore happily resigned to improvise Tybalt's name to T-Bo.

Kurt inspected the palm-sized fuzzball and predicted, "Thor will teach her."

I was incredibly encouraged with this wisdom and, of course, we spent T-Bo's weaning time together with Thor. Thor seemed equally distracted, being a two-year-old, between learning how to eat things weighing more than himself and teaching his protégé. In the end, Thor and T-Bo were in perfect alignment, and no man was safe! Frogs, lizards, even bugs, were eradicated! The occasional opossum left shredded on the neighbor's lawn! The school crossing guards in the neighborhood requisitioned chainmail, which of course the schoolboard denied. Through it all, Kurt and I only saw two dogs who loved us both, and would only cause whatever chaos we commanded.

T-Bo and I moved in with Kurt, Thor, and Kurt's girlfriend Tammy, to a chicken house converted into apartments on the now-busy Northlake Blvd. of old Palm Beach Gardens. Kurt and I diligently taught both dogs how to tree mailmen, chase garbage collectors, and otherwise warn us of any noise breaking the natural order of our environment. They were spectacular students. Kurt's brother, Steve, occupied the adjacent chicken coop with his dog Brutis, a 125-pound St. Bernard, and one evening we found all three dogs staring up in the Norfolk Island pine tree in the front yard.

Diane was the first one to see them and Steve's girlfriend yelled, "Steve, get Kurt and Keith!"

We found Steve's friend trembling in the branches, the dogs didn't even bark! We carefully extracted Steve's friend from the tree and I never saw him again.

I was now learning the lesson of economics the hard way. T-Bo and I moved back in with my parents and went to obedience school and technical college. We both earned our degrees. T-Bo practiced no better social skills, and I practiced marginally better technical skills, but we were both better prepared to adapt to our surroundings, and in our own ways, strive for greater goals. I was surfing every day for an hour or so before class, until the sun went down after school, and T-Bo was with me whenever I left the house.

My favorite surf spot was the reef behind the Hilton Hotel on Singer Island. The reef was the result of Mother Nature, and the wreck of the ship Amaryllis in 1965, three years after I was born. I want to describe the reef because it was the perch from which T-Bo observed her master for countless hours.

Some authority at the time hauled the wreck to the site situating it a mere twenty yards from the beach, probably long before the hotel was even built. Time and nature grew coral, channels, and currents around the foundered ship to present a reef situated just above the high-tide water line behind the hotel, with a natural reef situated several hundred yards to the north of that in front of the next condominium tower constructed waterfront. There was a county park in between the Hilton and the condominium. The two reefs created a cove in the county park to catch whatever swell that presented itself, and alter the break accordingly. Fantastic diversity in terms of surf options. When the swell was small and from the south, it lazily broke over the shallow north side of the Amaryllis. When the swell was from the easterly weather as usual, it broke over either side. But when there was a strong north swell, the natural reef to the north would break off a part of the swell, and the Amaryllis would break off the rest leaving a long peeling wave all the way to the beach south of the reef.

My friend Joe who lived on the island said, "K-Dude, you brought the hound."

"Always. Think Robin will be a sweetheart?"

"I don't know dude, you better have some sweet sugar or a pocket full of cash. Them girls run all over this island trying to keep up with that chaos. Last weekend she tipped over the popcorn machine at the Colonnades Hotel, then jumped in the pool. We had a three-girl posse on that one and Kim got tagged with the 'leash-law' ticket. You owe her $35. The Colonnades is two miles down the beach man, can you get it?"

"Yeah, I talked to Kim yesterday. I was taking a nap on the beach when she bolted. She'll be on the reef as soon as my board hits the water."

"Then you better start paddling if you ever expect to get laid again. And, you had better assign the direction of your maniac to one chick. It's not fair to the other girls."

"Shannon's in charge of that. Besides, all the girls love T-Bo."

"Yeah, but only two of them can keep up with her. Yesterday, Robin told Heather to arrest the puppy because she had a funny look. Before Heather could put a leash on her, T-Bo launched across the dunes toward A1A and so did Heather. The dog barked all personnel into their quarters at the Riviera Beach fire station. Heather managed to shake her ass enough to keep the fire-fighters from calling the cops but, dude, you're gonna get us kicked off the reef.

"Is Heather okay?"

"Dude, you don't get it! When you go into the water, the dog won't take her eyes off you. The minute you step on dry land, she rifles the camp to go wherever doggie dreams are made. The girls just can't keep up!"

This is where T-Bo grew up with my girlfriends and surf buds. She would swim with me as I paddled out to reach the break, then peel off to sit on the reef for hours just to watch my progress on the waves. She would not go back to the beach, and she would not be distracted by tourists on the reef in wonder of a dog in the middle of the ocean. She would carefully watch my movements among the waves and adjust her position on the reef to better observe me.

One day I picked up a wave, close and in front of the reef. As I read the wave, I knew I would have to pull my board high and tight on the lip of the curl to skirt the edge of the south point of the reef. I didn't make it. The tourist that pulled us off the reef said the wave had dropped suddenly from underneath me as the bottom of the wave hit the reef, and an opposing wave slapped me from behind. I got hauled across the reef on my back. She went on to say the dog watched it all coming, and was barking ferociously at the wave as it broke and swept her and myself across the reef. The very cute girl graciously dragged myself, my puppy, and my shattered surfboard, both of us bleeding, across the reef to calm water.

My friend Steve was standing at the shore, board under his arm as T-Bo and I waded across the shallow cut between the reef and the beach. He said, "K-Dude, that was a nice wave before you wrecked it."

Steve was staring at the tourist girl and I said, "The swell was strong this morning, now it's swinging around to the south, it'll crap out in two hours."

"You get her number?"

"Her dad's a Pratt & Whitney guy from Connecticut; she and her mom are at the Hilton for a month while he's out at Bee Line. You should go up to the pool and dazzle her. I got Shannon's number to worry about."

"Where's she at? She needs to be helping these girls."

"Dude, her mom's squeezing her about school. She's almost got a scholarship buttoned up. She can't get here too much."

"Well, she needs to. You know how funny you two look when you dress up? You look like a partially petrified leather-back turtle with yellow hair, and she looks like the icing on a vanilla cupcake!"

"And you look like a clown fish with a devious sneer!"

"So, like, does the vet patch up men, or the ER stitch up doggies, or do you have to make two appointments?"

"I'm not sure, but the one on my shoulder hurts. I gotta go."

"Later. You need vis-queen to cover your seats? There's some in the back of my truck."

"Thanks."

"T-Bo don't look so bad, but you got some dings. Your skull is bleeding, and your board's gonna weigh 35 pounds after you patch it up."

"I'll sacrifice it to mailbox duty and get a new one."

"A noble historical marker for all to see!"

Robin was the only girl who had a board and would paddle out with us. She was smoking hot! All the surf crew relentlessly pursued and harassed her. Because of this, I left her alone and she seemed to appreciate that. Robin verbally acknowledged this with gratitude, and she also acknowledged the sexual tension between us with Shannon to consider.

Robin was a strong woman, incredibly sexy, and knew exactly where she wanted to go. I was totally riding the fence on this one. Robin kind of took responsibility for my puppy if Shannon was not there. I never asked her to do that, she just kind of directed the other girls how to look after T-Bo when we were in the water. The only other girl who knew how to do that was Kim, but she was totally hands on; Kim would take responsibility for T-Bo even when Shannon was there. I cannot even begin to calculate the number of miles Kim chased T-Bo on Singer Island over the years!

T-Bo learned to be comfortable with the girls who came to watch us surf. They all became her surrogates and would feed, water, and entertain her while we surfed. I purchased a kite that T-Bo found fascinating. It was brightly colored with a streaming tail that T-Bo could not resist. I would set the kite out about 50 yards and stand at the shoreline. Another friend also named Kurt had a kite too, and we often would spend hours flying together if there were no waves. He would always inquire about the surf crowd, but he didn't surf. He would later become the "Best Man" at my wedding, but for the day he was designated the defensive coordinator for doggie jaws. The trapeze line would let me dip a wing wherever I wanted with the tail behind spinning precariously close to the ground, and T-Bo would dive after the kite, riffling anyone on site. T-Bo and I had cleared out about an acre of beachfront property, with which she could command my girlfriends, and keep watch with Kurt on me and my friends while we bobbed in the current.

One Saturday there was clean 3–5-foot crystal clear turquoise swell gracing us with a rare weekend appearance and the beach was packed. We had been here since sunup and I caught a wave to the beach to take a break about 11:00. As I paddled the last few strokes to shore, I watched T-Bo take off like a cheetah after an antelope heading straight down the shoreline toward public beach about a mile south of the Hilton. I watched Kim snatch up T-Bo's leash and take off after my puppy with Stacey right behind her.

I walked up to our beach camp and stuffed my board into the sand and grabbed a towel to dry off.

Robin said, "We should have a report in about an hour."

I grabbed a Gatorade from the cooler and took a seat on my towel and said, "Just wonder how much this one's gonna cost."

Sure enough, a little more than an hour later, T-Bo led Kim by the leash from the parking lot down the beach to our surf camp with Stacey and Darryl following. T-Bo curled up in the shade behind Kim's beach chair and went to sleep. I said, "What are the damages today?"

Kim said, "T-Bo wanted to go to 7-Eleven. She was there with Willie by the time we tracked her down."

Willie was a local guy who was the storekeep, and would feed T-Bo a package of peanut butter crackers every time we came for a beer run. Willie was an older black guy and he adored T-Bo. If he ever saw her unsupervised, he would tell one of the patrons to let her into the store, and he would keep her there until a posse showed up to retrieve her.

I asked Kim again, "What are the damages this morning?"

Kim said, "No casualties. I bought T-Bo an orange soda, and Darryl got her a Mars bar, Willie didn't charge us for her crackers, so you're in for $3.45. Darryl gave us a ride back."

I had only met Stacey a couple times. She was Kim's friend, and she asked, "Do you guys do this stuff every day?"

Robin said, "T-Bo kinda makes that decision every day."

I just looked at my puppy sound asleep in the shade of Kim's beach chair and tried to see Stacey's perspective. She was right, my puppy was crazy. Kim said, "Everyone on the island knows T-Bo. It's only the tourists that have to figure her out. They either love, or fear her, and when T-Bo smells fear, it gets interesting!"

Stacey said, "Then why don't you keep her on a leash here?"

The entire camp rang in unison, "Never!"

T-Bo would periodically swim out to the break to check on me. I would see her coming and couldn't help but chuckle at the girls' calls to retrieve her, and the dog's determination to be in my presence. I would hesitate to engage a wave and wait for her to reach the break. I would pull her up on the nose of my board to let her rest, and after catching her breath, I'd kick her off and we'd both find the next wave to the beach. You must understand, this was not only one day but our lifestyle for about six years. I have no idea where the dog learned how to swim.

One day after just such an episode, three of us were lined up beyond the break waiting for the next set.

Steve said, "K-Dude, you should get her a board and send her back to doggie school to learn how to paddle!"

R.D. said, "Naw man, a boogie board and frog flippers!"

I said, "Come on man, T-Bo knows the waves. And who do you think would have any fingers left if they tried to strap a leash or flippers on T-Bo's paws?"

Nothing!

One day my father took the family for a boating adventure to Peanut Island. As we were idling across the waterway, I noticed T-Bo the dog's ears prick up. She had sighted an inbound pelican bearing 345 degrees from the northwest cutting a flightpath immediately across our stern about three feet above the water. T-Bo leaped to the top of the motor housing lowering her front legs, butt in the air, crouched for the attack. I said "Hey, Dad…," but was paralyzed from action as I watched the snarling, barking, ballistic, frenzy in midair, with spastic fangs and claws bared to defend us from the offending foul. I could only shake my head as I witnessed the pelican drastically alter its flight plan then watch as my mom and sisters leaped up instantly considering jumping from the deck, and my dad bent over the helm in laughter. I simply watched as T-Bo landed with a big splash, fractionally missing her target, her frenzied barking gargling into silence as she submerged under the boat's wake. I just dove off the back of the boat to go get my puppy. I knew my dad would navigate the boat back around to retrieve us as I attempted to distract T-Bo from snorkeling.

ADJUSTMENTS

My folks got divorced when I was almost finished with my tech school. My dad had moved to Charlotte, North Carolina to take an engineering job and my eldest younger sister had moved away to college. I stayed home and began to build race cars in my dad's now-abandoned garage, and tried to be the man I imagined I must be for my mom and two other sisters. It was at this time that T-Bo's pack mates began to affectionately refer to her as Bebo. There was way too much estrogen in my world! So, I kept on surfing.

All my buddies and girlfriends seemed to alter their normal social schedules and were frequently visiting my mom's house in the evening to watch my progress with my cars. I had purchased a fire-burnt 72 Mercury Cougar convertible with a 351 Cleveland motor which I decided to build. I spent about $8,000 building the motor and tranny and put it right back in the busted-up Cougar.

Kurt's (Thor's dad) youngest brother Billy seemed to be the one most interested in my efforts. He would help me spec-out parts as I assembled the motor, and help me turn wrenches on the heavy stuff. Billy was much younger than me and I didn't understand his fascination with my own interests. It may have simply been for the friendship, because Billy never championed such a cause. He did however, stay for the duration of the project.

One night I asked him, "Billy, why are you over here every night getting filthy with me, instead of hanging with your bud's?"

"K, I know what they do, and there's no purpose in any of it."

Wow! I thought, *this from a seventeen-year-old.* "But dude, your missing all the chicks, the parties, all the fun, just to come here and work, get filthy, and stay up all night, while I don't pay you to do that. I don't get it."

"K-Dude, if you're spending this much money, this many hours, and this much effort, I'm sure there is something for me to learn here. I would rather be here than stewing with my buddies smoking dope." Again, this from a seventeen-year-old!

"Billy, just promise me you won't get hurt, and you won't patent my motor design."

"Keith, I'm loving this. I can't even fathom how you know all this stuff, but I see there's a process to it. I can't believe it's taking so long, but I understand it's an assembly, one thing after another, everything checked and double-checked. It's interesting. I want to see it work."

A third time, from a seventeen-year-old, "It's gonna work just fine, or we're gonna start over!"

I promptly wrecked my car precisely 501 miles after breaking the motor in, at about 170 MPH! Luckily, I landed in a canal instead of on the side of a bridge. I recruited a redneck buddy to retrieve my car from the canal at 3:00 a.m. with his 4-wheel drive, then I went to the hospital because my shoulder didn't work anymore. They made me hold five-pound sand bags with my arms down at my sides to take the x-rays.

After getting the car home, I purchased a 1970 Ford Pinto and began to install the 500 HP motor to replace the 4-cylinder powerhouse. All my buddies said I was crazy, but they were at my shop almost every night to watch me work, even the girls. I had the motor, tranny, cooling system, and firewall installed with the car on blocks waiting for the rear end from a Mustang from the junkyard to complete the project. Bebo loved this new enterprise of mine because it kept her entertained long into the evening with all of her friends.

Kurt's brother Billy stayed with me all the way though this. This kid had learned how to build precision race car motors and make structural modifications to a car chassis. He was always intimately interested in my own objectives, but he never went on to do a project of his own. I never really got that part, and I still wonder at his motive at the time. He has never offered one.

One day, Mom wanted Bebo and I to know that we would have to make a plan. She sat us both down and explained that she had sold the house, bought a condo, was moving there with my sisters, but Bebo, me, and my race cars were not invited. I blinked. Mom had strategically orchestrated this event to be in alignment with my graduation from tech school. This was pretty cool because it was my mom's way of getting me to think on a greater scale than, fish.

RELOCATION

I had to quickly dismantle the 500 HP Pinto and restore the car to operation with its original equipment. I added square yellow polka-dots, or polka-squares rather, and a throwing dart in the hood as my parting tribute to Palm Beach Gardens. I crated my hot-rod motor and stored it with the rest of my tools and nonessential belongings in a rented storage building. Of course, Bebo was curious as to what was going on because we were not spending time at the beach. Billy helped me with this endeavor as well, and was surprised at the quickness with which the transition came to its conclusion.

I made plans to join my dad in Charlotte, North Carolina. I asked my mom to care for Bebo while I moved up there and got settled into a place with my first professional job. Mom agreed to keep my puppy, but it was immediately evident this would not work. Bebo did not transition well. Anything under three feet tall was chewed to splinters by the doors to Mom's brand-new condo, there were torn screens if a window was open, rifled closets, shredded beds, cabinet doors unhinged, and no shoe left un-eaten. My puppy was a maniac. In just a few weeks she had left me, at the tender age of twenty-two, with some number like $10,000 in debt to my own mother. She lost fifteen of her forty-five pounds after I left just from separation anxiety. Mom promptly advised me that she would deliver my warm-blooded, black and tan responsibility to me at once.

Bebo arrived to find my two-acre mobile home site. She was comfortable there with neighboring kids to play with and woods to explore, and there was a train track on the north side of the property that disappeared into the forested North Carolina distance. Bebo and I both met Shelly, who was to become my wife and the only other person Bebo would ever take direction from. I remember Bebo's first challenge to this new female attracting my attention; Shelly came over for dinner one night and Bebo nipped her on the thigh when she was joining me on the sofa after dinner. Shelly jumped off me and walloped Bebo across the muzzle. The dog was shocked! Shelly effectively established herself as the matriarch in our little, as yet undefined, family, and this would play a significant role in my future decision-making. Bebo paid attention to Shelly, and I, paid attention to Bebo.

Bebo had long ago established her sea legs, but Shelly had not. One day, I took them both on a five-mile river run from my dad's house to a secluded rope swing that I knew about on the Catawba River. I beached the boat, and Bebo bounded instantly from the bow into the woods. Shelly and I commenced to love each other under the rope swing.

The tree to which the swing was attached leaned far off the river bank and would eventually fall into the river. It was a large oak or maple, I can't remember, but what I do remember is the easy climb up if you were the first guy there to retrieve the rope to swing. Shelly whispered that this was a great place to get to know each other, and I enthusiastically nodded my agreement.

Shelly said, "I never did this in the water before."

"There's lots of pools in Florida." I didn't tell her I hadn't either.

"There is no one in sight! We're outside! It's intimidating! It's hot!"

"Yeah, baby!"

We heard a peculiar scratching sound from above, and looked up to find my puppy, 30 feet up, and 20 feet out on a branch, chewing on the rope. I dutifully reprimanded the pup exclaiming, "Get down from there!" She obediently responded, launching off the branch, to land on Shelly at 160 MPH downward momentum. Mood broken, Shelly walloped Bebo across the muzzle (once again) and told her "Get in the boat!" There the dog lay snoozing in the bilge as I lazily navigated our way home. On the way, I was considering my psychotic puppy, and this woman who so easily took control over her. I knew I would later have decisions to make.

Bebo's next adventure was camping! Shelly and I had joined my dad and his girlfriend Jo Lyn (we called her Jo) at a campground in Carolina Beach just south of Wrightsville Beach, North Carolina. Dad pulled his rig into his designated slot and I pitched my well-traveled surf canvas at the site next door with the glorious new addition of an air mattress for my new girlfriend.

Jo Lynn was a very sensual older woman and I could see why my dad was attracted to her. She was genuinely interested in my relationship with Shelly. She had a comical habit of giggling when she was insinuating innuendo, and a pronounced Southern belle accent.

Jo said, "Keith, I've only met Shelly a couple times. Do you rilly think she's reeealy the one for you? He, hm, hm. She's soooo cute! He, hm. And how she just comaaaands Bebo! I just luv her to death."

"I don't know what to say, Jo, this is pretty new for me. Think she'll put up with a Florida boy?"

"I don't KNOW! I've been tryin' to figger that same thing bout your deddy! He, he, hm. Ya'll'r a differn't peeedigree, thet's fur sure!"

We went to dinner at a rustic old fish house with my dad and Jo, after carefully tethering Bebo to the utility pole with a long lead and surf-camp-sized bowl of water before we left.

When we returned after dinner, we saw that a new rig had pulled into the site next to ours while we were out. We could not see around the rig, but the strobes were making the crab cakes gurgle in my belly.

Dad said, "Uh-oh."

Nothing highlights the Carolina Coast in autumn like police lights and old men in boxers wielding cast-iron frying pans. We arrived back from dinner to find my puppy with a deflated canvass parachute behind her, pinning a man to his camper, and police with guns drawn! Once again, my father was bent over the helm in laughter as I leaped from the truck to mitigate the circumstances.

Jo said, "Eeead (my dad Ed), this ain't no laughin' matter!"

Shelly said, "Keith, don't get into a confrontation!"

"They're gonna shoot my puppy if I don't do something!"

"I'm coming!"

Shelly teased my puppy off the tourist as I engaged the police officers. The officers lowered their weapons as they saw Shelly subdue my puppy. The officers explained the weight of this situation and their requirement to uphold public safety. Bebo had broken the skin of this gentleman, and because of that my puppy was sent to quarantine until I could produce medical documents for her vaccinations.

Shelly never did enjoy the air mattress, sleeping instead that night on my chest on the dunes of the beach. I cannot say what taboo my Canadian neighbor broke with Bebo that evening at the utility pole, I only know that when I fished her lead from the wreckage, Bebo had kicked over her bowl of water, entered the tent clawing through a side window screen, chewed through the zippered front entrance, went around to another window and clawed back in, then exited the tent through a back window. She then pulled the whole package with tent stakes and poles, a deflated air mattress, coolers, and our clothes, to snarl the poor man back into his own camper. The man must have been terrified. Shelly somehow saw the humor, and simply said, "Your puppy's bad."

The next day was overcast with a misty kind of rain, no wind, and a lazy swell. I paddled out at first light, not so much to surf, but to think. When I had paddled beyond the break, I lay on my back on the board staring up into the gray sky, my legs dangling in the water. I was depressed. My thoughts of course presented every catastrophic direction my life may turn before I could figger out what to do with my hyper-metabolized, fanatically defensive, fiercely loyal, forty-five-pound tornado of a companion. It was at this time I realized I was thinking selfishly. I was concerned with the liability, cost, risks, inconvenience. I then considered the sacrifice my puppy was making for me, and it brought me to tears. Bebo was in prison!

BACK AT THE RANCH

Shelly helped me extradite my puppy from the New Hanover County legal system, and she repaired the damage to my surf camp. This was our first winter away from Florida, and both Bebo and I looked forward to the coming spring. Bebo was now a felon, and I assigned myself and Bebo to farm prep duty. Bebo happily rounded up the neighbor's kids to help, and she was particularly interested in the bunny pen I constructed in the middle of my one-acre garden site. Shelly's younger brother Robert seemed to be the leader of the neighborhood kids, and he assigned farm duties to the kids, and custodianship of my puppy to himself. I think we enjoyed a pepper and a couple ears of corn before abandoning the farm to the neighbors later that year.

There was a train track on the north side of my property and one day Bebo was investigating this area when I heard the unmistakable howl of pain. I jumped from my home with my 30/30 in hand in search of a target along the tracks. Luckily for them and for me, I did not find my target. But I did find my puppy winged around her shoulder blade pouring blood. Someone had used a knife to cut my puppy. It's funny how God works, I was so furious that someone could treat an animal like this that I was gonna gut shoot this guy. Then I would explain the error of his ways while he lay in pain, and then I was going to whip him to death with my gunstock. God let him go. I had to get my puppy to the doctor.

The doc put thirty-five stitches in Bebo and pumped her full of antibiotics.

Doc said, "Bebo is a peculiar patient. I would guess she typically wouldn't allow anyone to touch her but yourself. You don't have to bring her back if you can snip and pull the stiches. Give it ten days."

Bebo rebounded in two weeks as if nothing had happened. I did pull all Bebo's stiches myself, but I did not rebound with such grace. I felt as if my privacy had been violated with Bebo's injury, and I wanted the responsible party brought to bear. I interviewed neighbors introducing myself, and no one had witnessed anything in the area that day. I never did find them.

The next drama Bebo brought to my doorstep was quite literally, brought to my door step. I worked the 11–7 overnight shift as a process engineer at a cable manufacturing plant. One night I was finishing my dinner and getting ready for work while Bebo went out to relieve herself before I left. She did not respond to my calls for lights-out, and was off exploring the woods somewhere. I cussed her disobedience and the darkness, until I finally had to leave for work.

My neighbor across the railroad tracks was a taxidermist who I had only waved at in passing. When I returned from work at about eight the next morning, I arrived to find Bebo feverishly attempting to haul a three-foot-long deer leg haunch, backwards, up the stairway to my mobile home. She was covered with blood from muzzle to tippy toenails. Shelly lived just two houses away in a little clapboard cabin and just happened to be leaving for work at this time and she stopped to look. She just stared at me after looking at my puppy. When I turned to look at her, she had a quirky little smile, shaking her head. She did not say a word, just drove away. I was thinking of what time the taxidermist may leave for work!

I was tired, hungry, knew I had a spectacular mess to clean up, and would probably be hearing from the taxidermist at any time now. Bebo had left a blood trail leading from my neighbor's car port where the rest of the deer still lay, down the road and across the tracks, to end with splatter all over my front door. No forensics necessary here! The first thing I did, was dutifully retrieve my 30/30 and kept it perched by the front door.

Bebo and I then had an eye contact moment. She immediately started to growl as she knew I would then attempt to arrest the fresh member from her. I lurched for the hoof, and Bebo put a death clamp on the hip. I could hear her frenzied growling muffled around a mouthful of fur. We were now in a tug-of-war on the stairs and we both went tumbling off with the limb firmly in each other's grip. I could hear my neighbor Jerry howling in laughter across the street telling his wife Laura to get out there to watch the show. Bebo and I tugged it out, with snarling and expletives, across the lawn toward my Pinto in the drive. I was finally able to wrench the now shredded digit from my puppy, and strapped it onto my surfboard rack on top of the Pinto.

Jerry said, "Mister, I cain't figger Florida boys. Dat dog got you figgered out, but you's strugglin'! I told Laura 'Keep a watch,' but she cain't figger it either."

I said, "Jerry, my dog is a psychopath, I don't see any figgering here!"

"Check Bobby next door, he got 'dog whisperin' add-vice!"

"Thanks, Jer."

"See ya later, one of ya gonna git shot!"

"Jerry, I hope to make whatever restitution Mr. Fred demands, my puppy is crazy and I know it."

"Well, I just hope I see the lights on tonight. I'm gonna tell Laura to keep a check! We worried about ya boy!"

"Thanks, Jer. I'll check in with Bobby."

"Aah-ight then!"

Evidently, according to the neighbors, it was not uncommon for people to just drop dead animals in Mr. Fred's carport at any given hour. I never did see the taxidermist. I can only assume the deer's champion only wanted a trophy head mount for his office and was not concerned with the missing groceries.

I was exhausted. Bebo did several reconnaissance laps around the Pinto while I fetched the Palmolive dish soap and a leash. I thoroughly bathed the dog and myself in the freezing well house water by the garden. After her bath, before I could direct her back to the house, she went leaping for the bunny dung under the pen in the middle of the garden to dry off. Shaking my head, I went back in the house to get another leash. Then, with my puppy securely fastened to the plumbing, I bathed her again. Then I went on to scrub my front door, staircase, patio, car, riffle…

…I awoke that evening about eight to find Bebo comfortably draped over Shelly's lap on the sofa watching TV and waiting for me. As soon as I entered the room, I heard Bebo's tail rhythmically thumping, and I saw that exact same quirky smile. Shelly said, "So, tell me about your day."

I explained to Shelly my anxiety at not understanding why my puppy seemed to "choose," "when," to be disobedient. I could not for the life of me, figure that out! It created tremendous disruption in my planning process.

Shelly said, "It's because you need to demonstrate to her who's the one in charge."

"Shelly, that's ridiculous, the dog's seven years old! Bebo knows what's up."

"I don't have any problem with Bebo."

"I've noticed. What would your enlightened counsel be to a Florida cracker boy?"

"Be consistent. Bebo knows I treat her the same way in every circumstance, with a muzzle shot if she doesn't respect me. I command, she obeys, or muzzle shot. Get it?"

"I guess, but I was always surfing while that stuff was happening on the beach with Bebo. Guess I never learned. Ever give her a bloody nose?"

"Nope. It's really just a swat, but it immediately gets her attention, and she understands instantly that I'm not happy with whatever is rolling around in her doggie brain."

"Shit!"

The next event Bebo brought to my life was truly scary. Someone shot Bebo. Once again, Bebo ran off while I was preparing to head out for work, and once again I cussed the woods and darkness (and myself) for her disobedience. Luckily, this was a Thursday night which meant that after my shift I was off until Sunday evening. When I got home from work Friday morning I found my puppy in obvious discomfort on the front steps. I searched my puppy from stem to stern looking for damage. I found her clean and intact except for a spot on her rear end about the size of a fingernail that was glazed over on her right rear thigh.

She favored this leg somewhat, and seemed not to want to settle. I observed Bebo for about an hour and decided we needed to see the doc because the weekend was upon us and I knew she was hurt inside. Bebo did not try to eat the lead blanket or the x-ray technician so I knew she was in pain and that made me worry all the more. Sure enough, doc saw what he thought we would find as a .22 caliber load lodged in Bebo's chest after traveling from behind through all her guts. He gave Bebo doggie-dope, split her sternum to belly button, and went to work stitching her up. He worked for hours and when Bebo finally started to flat-line on the dog-o-meter, doc stitched her closed and explained to me that he had followed the bullet's path from Bebo's thigh, stitching and cleaning every perforation along the way to find the bullet lodged between Bebo's lungs. He could not remove it without disturbing the lungs and heart and did not think she could make it through that surgery. He explained that her body would develop a fibrous cocoon around the bullet, and that he had patched up the rest of her internal injuries. I would now become Bebo's caregiver and Bebo was not a patient patient. Somehow, I could not bring myself to deliver the recommended muzzle shot for her disobedience.

A CHANGE OF SCENE

Bebo already knew I was hopelessly in love with Shelly, and Shelly knew I loved my puppy. We were a family and had to figger out how to make it work, and the girls seemed to know this before I even considered it. I am afraid of no man, but I cannot hunt men. However, I could otherwise change my circumstances so they couldn't hunt me either. Bebo's injury demonstrated to me that someone close to my home would shoot from behind. That's scary. How could I protect my two girls if someone would shoot from behind? I made arrangements to move in with a buddy from work and we abandoned the garden to my neighbors. I wanted to see if this separation would test my feelings for Shelly. It did, and she was still the love of my life (I did not tell her this at the time). Bebo, me, and eventually Shelly, happily settled in with my friend Brian in Fort Mill, South Carolina, just over the border from Charlotte, North Carolina.

Brian said, "Keith, do you reckon Dana will git along with Bebo and Shelly?"

Dana was Brian's girlfriend who was only causally committed to the relationship, so I wasn't so concerned other than to consider my friend's circumstances. We had a financially binding relationship with understood terms, but I had no idea what terms he held with Dana.

I told Brian, "Look, at the end of the day, it's me, Shelly, and Bebo living here, you and Dana dating here. We all have to get along. So, can we do that?"

Brian later told me he didn't hold much confidence in the relationship, and was reasonably sure we would be just fine. Bebo was the deciding factor in Brian's relationship with Dana. One day when Shelly and I were at work, and Brian was entertaining Dana, Bebo decided to go on laundry duty. She chewed up multiple pairs of Dana's panties! Brian tried to salvage the event saying he would take her shopping for new ones. Dana was furious. To Brian's credit, he did not blame me or Bebo for this infraction, he rather inflected that Dana was not committed! and that the event was quite comical! I was grateful for this forgiveness, and Brian and I still enjoy a healthy relationship. Bebo recovered quickly and gracefully from the gunshot and got ready for her second winter away from Florida.

One night at work, they informed us that by the time we left in the morning there would be a foot of snow in the parking lot. I was from Florida! What was I to do with a foot of snow?

A couple of buddies that also worked in the engineering department had a lot of fun at my expense that night. Cyril, Dennis, and I were calibrating the new equipment installed on one of the extrusion lines at the plant. Cyril was a middle-aged guy from Ireland or Scotland, I'm not sure which, but his accent was pronounced. Dennis was a guy about my age who graduated from MIT in Massachusetts.

Cyril said, "Keith me lad! Did they teach ye to navigate winter weather in driver education class in ye home state of Florida?"

Dennis said, "Are you kidding Cyril? Florida has one of the lowest educational ratings in the nation! They would never include such nonessential curriculum to their budget!"

"With such a low rating, how'd ye fellow secure employment with the likes such as we here at Siemens?" Cyril wanted to know.

Dennis said, "Well, Keith knows his digital and mechanical well enough, so I guess he learned something in Florida. And his grades must have been good enough, or he wouldn't have gotten the interview. Maybe the corporate guys hired him for exactly this reason; to see how a Florida boy does when it snows. I bet they all got wagers on him calling out tomorrow night with car problems. Think I'll follow him home in the morning just to watch!"

"I'll follow ye following 'im!" Cyril said.

Cyril and Dennis kept bantering back and forth until we finished our work, and I kept my mouth shut and let them have their fun. I'm sure they were disappointed when I didn't bite on their antics. I genuinely liked Cyril, and enjoyed his endless description of the old country on our downtime. Dennis and I were good friends and played tennis whenever our schedules allowed.

I wrecked my Pinto seven times into all sorts of different stuff on the five-and-a-half-mile drive home, even scraping off some of my polka-squares. When I got there to let Bebo out, she bounded off the porch to land knee-deep in snow and stopped promptly looking back over her shoulder for an explanation. She did not move. I made a snowball and took aim at her face.

I smiled at her and yelled, "Get the bunny," and whipped the snowball straight into her mouth. She chomped it and took off like a mink in the January Yukon forest. I waited about an hour for Bebo to finish her survey of the snow-covered premises and kindly retrieve three pecans, then Shelly pulled up. She announced she had taken the day off and wanted me to know she intended to teach a Florida boy how to survive a winter, and then told me to put my puppy away.

I said, "Sit!"

Shelly did, in fact, teach me. For hours, I was intensely studying "Advanced Winter Survival Tactics" when Bebo, ever-curious, poked her cold wet nose in exactly the wrong curve on Shelly's bottom. Shelly leaped off me, screeching at Bebo, bounding for the door with my jeans in her hand to whip the dog. Bebo playfully led Shelly a lap around the coffee table before crashing out the patio door, off the porch. Shelly was hot on her tail.

I was pulling up my boxers and putting on my socks, as I was hearing lamps falling, furniture moving, ferocious barking, female blasphemy, and finally a door blasting open. I walked out onto the patio to find the two women, who were most important in my life, face-to-face, knee-deep in snow, and growling at each other, naked!

Shelly was almost hyperventilating with her long, dirty blonde hair in disarray, dragging my jeans in one hand through the wet snow, my puppy was panting. I remember thinking how I was gonna spin this event to my neighbors, who were out shoveling driveways, scraping their car windows, looking at me. I yelled commandingly to my neighbors, "She was in the shower!" The dog seemed to smile at this and so did I. After warming up a little, and locking my puppy securely in the garage, Shelly returned so I could re-take my final exam in "Advanced Winter Survival Tactics!"

SOUL SEARCH

Bebo probably didn't know that she had become God's tool to teach me to love more deeply and broadly. Not long after Bebo's only experience with snow, my company announced it would close the Charlotte operation and move key products to the headquarters in Hickory, North Carolina. At once, I knew I would return to Palm Beach County, but I now had some serious thinking to do.

Bebo and I spent the rest of the winter taking long forays in the woods while I wrestled with the decision I had to make. The plant would close in a few months and I had not yet told Shelly.

When I left Florida after graduating, I also left a lasting high school relationship with Shannon, who was Bebo's primary surrogate mother. Shannon is the one responsible for teaching Bebo how to climb trees while I was surfing! Shannon and I rationalized at the time that it was best to just break our relationship. Long distance seldom worked, I could not take her with me, and it was not fair to have any other expectations. It was painful at the time and I have always regretted that decision.

I did not want to make this same mistake with Shelly. I knew that if I invited Shelly to come with me, I would marry her. What I did not know is, did she hold this same conviction? I sat for many hours with Bebo in the woods. I did not want to lure Shelly away from her family, I didn't want give her any false hopes about our future prospects, I did want her to know how I felt, but I didn't know how to present my feelings. I wanted to know her reciprocating feelings. What finally snapped me from my mood was watching Shelly attempting to arrest my puppy from riffling the baskets of my neighbor's Easter egg hunt for the kids.

That evening, while Shelly coaxed a Pez dispenser from Bebo's fangs, applied nail polish remover to remove the Peeps goo from her ears, claws, muzzle, and eyes, and carefully brushes egg shells away, I explained how I felt.

I told Shelly about the plant closing. I told her of all my concerns regarding my fears and hopes. I told her of my love for her. Shelly did not interrupt me. She paid rapt attention as she administered care for my puppy. When I was finished, she did not say a word. She threw my puppy off her lap, dragged her to the confines of the garage then pulled me immediately to the bedroom to study proper sexual etiquette during the spring equinox! We went to Florida.

HOME AGAIN

I had made arrangements for Bebo, Shelly, and me to land at my sister's home with her husband and daughter. Of course, the first place I took Shelly to visit was my favorite surf spot at the reef. It was a Tuesday morning and the beach was all but deserted. Bebo gleefully bounded into the sand and ran for miles chasing sandpipers and ghost crabs, the occasional tourist. She was so elated with joy to be home that she seemed to randomly wiggle periodically as she pounced along the beach, as though her wiggling were an involuntary motor skill.

Shelly waded out to the first coral reef she had ever seen as I sat quietly at the shore reflecting on my past and the new responsibilities I had now imposed on myself. I thought of Bebo's love, devotion, and protection of me, and of her suspicious observation of anyone who addressed me, and of her unconditional trust in me to see to her well-being. I also thought of Shelly's incredible strength, demanding obedience from my stunningly puzzled and frustrated K-9, of her efficiently applying her decision-making and organizational skill to all aspects of our collective life, and of her obvious adoration and trust in me. As the weight of all this settled on me, I smiled, and swam out to join my beautiful wife-to-be on the reef, with Bebo quickly crashing into my wake to follow.

There were no waves this day and the water was calm, crystal clear, and the same turquois color as Shelly's eyes. We spent the whole day here where I taught Shelly how to snorkel and fend off sharks, barracudas, sting-rays, and puppy claws.

We spent the next weeks and months securing employment, finding an apartment, giving Shelly a tour of Palm Beach County, and introducing her to the rest of my friends and family. It was at this time, the novelty of a new and exciting life-change in a beautiful place was wearing off for Shelly, and we settled into our new lifestyle. One night after work as we routinely went about our evening, I noticed Shelly's mood dejected and quiet. I quietly waited for an explanation that did not come. After a light dinner, I went to my chair to read and could hear Shelly quietly tinkering back in the bedroom.

After a short time, I registered Shelly approaching, and looked up to watch her address me with her head down and tears streaming down her lovely face. It was the first time I had ever experienced her crying. Shocked into alarm, I embraced her with my whole body and asked her what was wrong. She returned the embrace, melting into me, and continued to quietly whimper and shudder for so long that I began to panic. After standing together a few minutes, I led her to the sofa and pulled her into another embrace on my lap with her face buried in my shoulder where she continued to cry.

Shelly's courage asserted itself after only a few more minutes, and she began to calm and breathe. I was suffering serious anxiety over the explanation I was about to hear; my mind was racing with every failure or infraction I could possibly have penalty for, or what demon could have so possessed her. After a final steadying breath, Shelly said, "Keith…," Shelly explained that she felt overwhelmed and intimidated. She was intimidated with my easy relationships with my friends when she had none, she was intimidated by the beautiful girlfriends of my past which we joined at the beach each day and she felt in competition with each of them, she felt intimidated by attempting to care for Bebo and me according to my family's expectations. She also explained to me that she considered these emotions to be a personal weakness that she was afraid to bring to our relationship.

I was truly drowning in devastation as I listened to Shelly honestly and humbly share her fears with me. I'm quite sure she felt my heart rate rise as I acknowledged my failure to anticipate this possible response from her in moving to this new environment, and I was furious at myself for that. I spent the next several hours honestly allaying each one of her fears in turn with long conversation. Most importantly, I explained that her personal friendships would come at her own discretion, and that there was no competition with anyone; I had chosen her as the champion before we even came here. Shelly was tremendously relieved after our hours-long session and we both slept soundly that night. She seemed to have dismissed the whole event by the next day, but I spent days considering how to apply Shelly's emotions to my social and family posture. The solution did not take days, it took years.

BANSAI THE BIRD

As Shelly got more comfortable in her new environment, the novelty reasserted itself to some extent, and she began to enjoy some new friends and the South Florida environment. We went with a few friends to a Thursday evening art show at a local marina to enjoy dinner, drinks, and local art vendors with kiosk displays along the waterfront docks.

After dinner, we and our friends strolled among the vendors to shop. I don't think any of us intended to patronize any of the offerings, but it was a lovely evening, and a laid-back atmosphere.

There was one vendor that caught Shelly's attention, and she pulled me by the hand to go see. The guy was dressed in pirate garb and had a display of several cages of exotic birds and several free-standing perches with juvenile Quaker Parrots on them.

Quaker Parrots have a brilliant bright lime-green back, with a gray belly and an attractive parrot beak. The adults typically reach a height of about 12 inches. Shelly was completely taken by the birds as the vendor assisted her in handling several of them and demonstrating their vocabulary skills. I was pleasantly amused by Shelly's fascination and curious where this would lead her mind in negotiating with the vendor.

The vendor, as it turns out, was a veterinarian and he gave Shelly his card. The vet went on to explain to Shelly that Quakers were quite trainable and had an excellent potential for vocabulary. He explained that the best way to husband a Quaker was to acquire an infant, and train it on a perch rather than in a cage. He said that as the infant's pin feathers came in, she should keep them trimmed to discourage the bird from flight, and encourage it to pedestrian mobilizing and social interaction.

I was sitting on a bar stool at the kiosk while I listened to this interaction. After Shelly finished asking all her questions, I had a big smile on my face when she turned to ask for my blessing.

Shelly said, "Keith, I want to try this. We have Bebo, but she is yours, not mine. I think I can do this. Will you let me try?" smiling brightly. I knew this is exactly what was going to happen.

"My sweet, I'm your companion, not your keeper. Make whatever decisions you wish, and know that I will support them."

"Oh Keith! I'm going to love this bird! I'm going to teach it how to talk, and how to behave! And they're so pretty. We can build a perch for the breakfast nook! The bird will love it there in front of the window! Thank you! Thank you! Thank you!"

"You will need to negotiate the price with Captn' vet-boy over there." The vet had left us alone to make the decision; he was fussing with all of the cages and perches.

Shelly said, "How much does an infant Quaker cost?"

The pirate said the price was $400.

Shelly asked, "Where did you get the parrots?"

The vet said, "From an importer in Miami."

Shelly then advised the vet, "Then I will need the importation documents to register the bird with my own veterinarian. Where are they from anyway?"

The vet said, "Well, I kinda got a deal for them with no documents. How about half price at $200? I have no idea where they're from."

Shelly said, "You're not a veterinarian, you only play one on Thursday nights. I'll give you $25 for one of your birds."

The pirate held his hand out and smiled, saying, "Done."

I busted out laughing and so did Shelly and the pirate. The guy went on to seriously teach Shelly about caring for the bird. He was quite knowledgeable about husbanding birds, and Shelly felt confident in her ability to care for it.

I asked Shelly, "What are you going to name this pink, featherless, por-cupine-looking-like, bird?"

Shelly said, "I'm going to name him Bansai. If I have to clip his feathers, he will crash every time he tries to fly. It just seems right."

I kissed Shelly and smiled.

When we got home, Shelly made a shoe box nest for the little guy and kept it on the kitchen counter for a couple days. I built a perch stand to fit nicely in the breakfast nook as Shelly had suggested. It had a shallow wooden pan as a base that was about two feet square with a plywood bottom. Around the plywood, I used teakwood trim to create a casing as the sides of the pan about 1 ½ inches deep. I then applied clear urethane sealer so the pan was cleanable and presented a nice finish on the teakwood casing. The result was a two-foot square wooden cookie sheet about 1 ½ inches deep. I mounted the pan to a piece of cypress stump about six inches in diameter and used pieces of the root base to create heavy, stubby legs to stabilize the stand. I cut the top of the stump to length such that the pan was at waist height.

Then I took Bebo for a seek and find mission in my truck. I had a Toyota SR-5 4x4 and Bebo and I went to an accessible area to the intracoastal water-way just north of the Bluffs development in Jupiter. I chose this location to search for seasoned driftwood to complete Bansai's perch with attractive branches for him to play on.

When I left Florida, this development was not even here. This is where my buddies and I brought our girlfriends to ride our off-road toys, 4x4s, and have our bonfire parties. We dubbed the place "Ski Beach." On weekends, 4x4s lined the beach side by side, lawn chairs and coolers filled the shore line, ski boats, jet skis, and every other imaginable vessel were anchored just off shore, and kids, pets, lovers, and families would all have their respective camps in order. I was disappointed that the development had consumed well over half of my old stomping grounds.

I pulled into the first trail leading back to the intracoastal waterway. The landscape was sand dunes filled with palmetto stands, scattered miniature pine areas, a few skimpy cypress stands, and scattered mangroves at the waterway. Bebo was quite accustomed to the drill: "get-out-of-the-cab, lock-in-the-4x4 hubs, and stay-in-front-of-the-truck-where-I-can-see-you!" We proceeded down the trail at 5–15 miles per hour, rolling up, over, and around all the landscape. The sand was like sugar, and I had to keep enough momentum to not bog down. Bebo was just kind of trotting as I followed behind her, her tongue lolling. After only ten minutes or so, we parked my truck at the most northern area of ski beach where the mangroves began along the waterway. I got out of the truck and Bebo and I started hiking.

As I began my search, it was comical to watch Bebo precede me assuming to know where I was going. She would find a colony of fiddler crabs, and attempt to pounce them before they could disappear into their holes. She would watch as they re-appeared out of the hole, and attempt to pounce them again. I sat for about a half an hour to observe this behavior. I think Bebo may have had OCD! She also found a family of opossums living in the mangroves as we navigated north, and to my surprise, she did not attempt to molest them, but she was intent on investigating them.

We then came to a tide pool where a sand bar retained water that led a hundred yards or so away from the intracoastal. As we approached, I could see a rather large snook trapped in the pool at low tide with a narrow sand bar preventing his escape into the intracoastal. The pool was only knee deep until the tide came up.

I used to take Bebo to a river-rock spillway on a small stream in the woods that eventually lead to a local golf course. The water on the upstream side of the spillway was the color of dark molasses from the countless cypress trees in the woods. After lazily trickling through the river-rock spillway, there was a clear pond with a river-rock bottom on the downstream side. I would select a rock and show it to Bebo, then toss it into the pond asking her to fetch it. She would gaze upon the thousands of similar rocks, then plunge her head under water in search of the right one! She would slowly blow bubbles out of her nose looking at the floor of the pond and select a rock to bring to me. One time, I had my .22 rifle and fired a shot into the pond only to watch Bebo crash into the pool to retrieve the bullet. Of course she could not find it, but she blew bubbles from her nose in search of the object that had caused the tiny plop in the water. I suppose this was one of the many swimming skills Bebo employed when we were surfing.

At the tide pool, Bebo spotted the fish, and began to cautiously stalk it. I found a small cypress tree to lean back on to watch this hunt. The snook could see Bebo and assumed a boundary. If Bebo moved closer, the fish moved away. Bebo circled the fish learning this boundary, and finally began lunging at the fish from all angles to catch it. The fish tired quickly in the confines of the pool and Bebo finally latched on to its tail and began to drag it to the sand bar. As the water got shallow, the fish spun around to latch on to Bebo's front leg. Bebo yipped, let go, and then began the dance again.

I knew this challenge would keep Bebo's attention for quite some time, so I continued on my mission to collect driftwood. I returned to the tide pool after about a half an hour to find Bebo on the sand bar still stalking this fish. All four of her ankles were bloody, and she had a missing patch of fur on her muzzle, and she was panting.

I said, "That fish got a can of wup-ass, huh?"

Bebo kind of looked around for a minute with that "stressed-out puppy" expression on her face, and I could not help but to laugh at her!

I said, "Get in the truck!"

Bebo bounded off the sand bar and went sprinting for the truck. I had a nice bundle of driftwood to present to Shelly for consideration of completing Bansai's perch. Bebo drank almost a whole gallon of water after fighting the fish when we got to my truck. I just watched and thought, what could possibly drive this dog to do what she does? What really had me concerned, is that I knew I now had to introduce her to a bird that she was not allowed to eat!

Shelly selected the driftwood she wanted to finish the perch. I fastened the pieces to the base pan and to each other to create a gymnasium for Bansai to navigate, and the branches rose to about five feet in height. I trimmed the branches such that they did not allow Bansai access beyond the base pan, and Shelly hung some toys for him to play with. We filled the bottom of the pan with corn cob grinds to act as kitty litter, and we waited for Bansai to mature.

DOG MEETS BIRD

I want to remember that only a couple weeks later Bansai lost the last few of his pin feathers and began to bounce around his shoe box until he started chewing out of it. Shelly transferred him to the perch and spent diligent hours teaching him where his food and water bowls were situated. She had to train him not to screech when we didn't pay attention to him. It was when Shelly made this transfer, that Bebo associated the new critter smell in our apartment to the visual detection of a bird.

I arrived home one evening to find Shelly and Bebo seated at the breakfast nook in front of Bansai's perch. Shelly was deep in conversation with Bebo, though I could not hear the context, nor did I wish to interrupt them.

After quite some time in discussion, Shelly retrieved the bird on her finger and presented it to Bebo. Bebo of course was curious and nervous. As Shelly drew the bird closer to Bebo's nose, Bebo took a couple of sniffs, then her left upper lip started to quiver. Of course Shelly was watching for exactly this reaction, and she swatted Bebo across the muzzle saying, "No!"

Bebo trotted away to come lay down at the foot of the reading chair where I was sitting, observing this training session.

Shelly demanded, "Get back over here!"

Bebo slowly swaggered back to the perch and Shelly commanded, "Sit!"

Bebo obeyed. Shelly demonstrated multiple presentations of Bansai to Bebo with only one more muzzle shot. I sat in my reading chair observing this educational technique. Shelly finally came over to flop in my lap and said, "There!" pointing to Bebo sitting still as a mannequin at Bansai's perch with the bright green bird standing on top of her head, "now we understand each other!"

Shelly said, "C-mere Bebo!"

Bebo gave a half shake of her head sending Bansai flapping to the floor and bounded for the chair. Shelly praised and scratched Bebo all over, then pointed and said, "That's my bird! You better take good care of him."

Bansai came slowly toodling toward us, and Bebo seemed to have one of those nervous doggie grins on her face.

BONDING

Bansai's antics with Bebo were truly surprising and laughable without fail, I never knew what to expect every time the bird approached the dog. Shelly spent many patient hours teaching Bansai his vocabulary, and the circumstances and times at which he chose to voice his opinion were utterly hilarious. Bansai's voice had a rather surprisingly deep tone compared to his natural screech. Whenever Shelly, I, and the animals were spending family time together, Shelly would always encourage Bansai to MC the show.

Shelly would say things like, "Bansai, tell Bebo what to do."

Bansai would respond, "Walk the plank, swabby!" and do a little head bobbing dance.

Spectacular!

Over time the animals did, in fact, bond in some unknowable way. The best description I can give is respect. One of Bebo's strides was like three miles of Bansai steps, so Bebo was never in danger of being accosted by the bird, but Bansai enjoyed being in the dog's presence and would find or follow her around the house. I find it funny that their moods at any given time would clearly make it apparent who was the aggressor and who was the victim in the interaction, but not once was there any violence. Usually Bansai was the aggressor, but occasionally Bebo would approach his perch to find him napping on a branch and she would punch his perch with her nose to see if he would fall off!

Bansai was the one who typically initiated playtime. He would quite ungracefully flap down to the floor from his perch and go toodling around the house in search of his puppy. He knew where Bebo's favorite napping spot by my reading chair was, and would always check there first. Sometimes I would find them both napping there with Bebo laying on her side dozing, and Bansai standing on her collar with his eyes shut also dozing, it was a comical sight to see.

Shelly had attempted to teach Bansai the entire oration of "Peter Piper." Bansai learned all the words, but he would recite them in whatever order he chose to be appropriate for the situation. "Pickled Peter." "Peck of Piper," "Pickles pick?"

One Sunday I was watching a ballgame when I noticed Bansai flap to the floor in search of his puppy. He would take several steps forward, stop, head bob, continue. This attitude continued until he came around the sofa to find Bebo, sound asleep, by my chair. Shelly wasn't at home.

Instead of crawling up Bebo's front leg to stand on her collar as he usually did, Bansai walked, head bobbing all the way, to address Bebo's nose within an inch. Bebo was still sound asleep.

Bansai yelled at the top of his lungs, in that deep throat tone, "PICKLED PEPPER!" Bansai never used the "s" to make it plural.

Bebo pogo-sticked off the floor from a dead sleep, and Bansai madly flapped his wings to escape the thirty-five-hundred-foot-tall predator screeching frantically. This pissed Bansai off. He began to sprint as fast as bird legs will go toward Bebo.

"PICKLED PEPPER, PICKLED PEPPER, PICKELD PEPPER, PICKELED PEPPER!"

Bebo was quite concerned with this development, and moved away.

"PICKLED PEPPER, PICKLED PEPPER!"

She headed for the hallway. Bansai was going as fast as he could go to catch her.

"PICKLED PEPPER, PICKLED PEPPER, PICKLED PEPPER, PICKLED PEPPER!"

"Yip"

"PICKLED PEPPER!"

Bansai ran out of gas and started toodling back to his perch.

Un-fucking-believable! My life was in serious need of an adjustment.

BOOM

Bebo doesn't like fireworks. In my experience, no dog likes fireworks. Hound dogs will put up with them, but generally, if it goes *Pow* dogs will run like any other animal. And, Bebo has good reason to fear a *bang*; after all she was shot—twice.

I decided without consulting Shelly, that I would tame Bebo's fear, making plans with some buddies to meet at the golf course to watch the Fourth of July show.

Shelly said, "Why are you bringing Bebo!"

"Because I want her to realize she can be with us in a stressful event and be okay."

"You're crazy!"

We met our buddies at a restaurant parking lot close to the 16th green. There were girlfriends, a couple of infants, and one other dog, a beagle. We all laid out our blankets and coolers on the green, and it was getting close to sunset. Bebo was already panting and nervous from the random *Pops* all day.

Shelly admonished me, "I know this can't be a good idea."

"Baby, if we keep her calm through this, she'll realize it's okay."

I had situated our blanket on the ruff of the green and planted an umbrella to fend off the last of the evening sunrays. I tied Bebo's leash to the base of the umbrella, and she did a couple of laps around it before settling down on the blanket. We sat and enjoyed our company for a while, and Bebo calmed down in spite of the few *pops* from bottle rockets and kids lighting firecrackers.

After an hour or so, the country club sent up a couple of ticklers and Bebo perked her ears up and started panting again. An instant later, *KA-BOOM!* a mortar sent an atomic blast that launched Bebo off of Shelly's flowered comforter. Her leash took the umbrella with her and left a rake of destruction across every camp along the 17th and 18th fairways toward the clubhouse.

I was sprinting as fast as I could go, and finally caught up to her at the command center where the show had stopped, and the firemen in charge were trying to corral Bebo and her umbrella. I went over and settled Bebo, and Shelly was just arriving. The firemen were saying things like, "Who brings a dog to the fireworks?" or "Whose ____ing dog is this?"

That's when Bebo went crashing down the line of mortars lined up on the 1st fairway with her umbrella in tow. Shelly yielded her off the line as two firemen held me by the elbows. I tried to explain to the officers that we were trying to wean my puppy from her fear, but they just cussed me for interrupting the show.

With the umbrella discarded and Bebo securely in tow, Shelly met me with the firefighters. She said, "I don't think there's any crime here, can you please let my boyfriend go." The firemen let me go while Bebo was snarling at them and Shelly gave her a muzzle shot.

On our long walk back to the parking lot, *Thwack!* Shelly swatted me on the neck with the end of Bebo's leash. She exclaimed, "I'm tired of chasing you and your puppy! You both need to knock this shit off! I'm not doing this anymore!"

I said, "Baby, we don't do it on purpose. At least I don't. Thank you for keeping us out of trouble."

Thwack!

"Oowww!"

"I'm telling you, Keith, You're on your own! Bebo needs to graduate into middle-age. You two are stressing me beyond my capacity!"

"I'm sorry baby, give me a hug."

Thwack!

"Oowww!"

"Don't touch me!"

I have always been an early riser, and the mocking bird has always been an icon of the great state of Florida. Typically, I will rise between four or five without the alarm, cook a pot of coffee, and wait for the dawn. I cherish this time each day and consider it as God's personal blessing to my life. Of course, Bebo would be at my heel as soon as I moved, so she and I would go out to the patio for some hours of solitude and reflection only to be joined by the mocking birds at this early hour.

After relieving herself, Bebo would join me in quiet contemplation on the patio, studiously watching the darkness from my work bench. We would listen to first one, then several mocking birds engage in nature's morning conversation. *"Chew chew whipper whipper whip trill trill trill."* From my tree.

"Tweeter tweeter tweeter whip whip chew chew chew whip." From a few doors down.

"Whipper whipper tweet tweet tweet whoooooo." Across the street.

On and on this conversation would go until the dawn would expand it to many other participants. Shelly and Bansai would join us around seven, sleepy-eyed and quiet. I can imagine the mocking bird's conversation:

"Good morning, Elizabeth, what are you doing today?"

"I want to go to the lake before it gets too hot."

"I saw a bunch of dragonflies there yesterday." From across the street.

Shelly and Bansai would slowly wake up on the patio with Bebo and me, and without words, we would say "good morning" to each other. Eventually, Bansai would let out a loud *schreech* and flap to the floor to go see his puppy. This would put a stop to the mocking bird chatter, and Bebo and Bansai would plan their day.

NEW ADDITIONS

My sister Vicki and her future husband Vince moved in with us so we could all save a little money. We had a very large and comfortable two bedroom, two bath duplex with a fenced yard that Bebo, Shelly and I did not begin to take advantage of. We were two young, working, couples with one psychotic puppy to manage; it didn't seem insurmountable and my sister and Vince were quite accustomed to Bebo's escapades, having heard all about medical expenses, court costs, damages….

Shelly had been in conversation for some time with her mother about us taking custodianship of her youngest brother JD. He was fifteen years her younger and was about ten years old in fifth grade when he joined us with Vince and Vicki. The boy already knew Bebo from my time in North Carolina and was happy to be reunited with her. Bebo proved to be the best babysitter we could have acquired. She distracted the boy from his hooligan peers, and was fiercely protective of him. He would jump on his skate board and put a leash on Bebo. I would see them all over the neighborhood doing Mach 2 down the streets as Bebo navigated with her tongue flapping over her shoulder.

One day shortly after JD's arrival, Shelly announced to me that my next, now high priority, domestic project was to build a doghouse and run-line for Bebo in the fenced yard; she explained that there was no way on God's green earth that she would attempt to keep house for Vicki, Vince, and ourselves, with a ten-year-old boy, and a prophetically imaginative Dobie-Lab in her presence. I'm sure I admitted a few worry lines across my brow, but I began at once to design Bebo's new apartment.

Bebo, JD, and I procured materials from the marine supply store and the lumberyard, and in short order had Bebo's new condominium beautifully constructed. It was a cute Key West bungalow design, with gingerbread trim. I ran a hundred foot, stainless steel sailboat shroud 8 feet high across the yard from corner to corner, securing it with turn-buckles at either end to keep tension on the shroud. To this, I tethered a 15-foot lead with a snap-shackle on the shroud, and one for Bebo's collar. This configuration gave Bebo the entire run of the side yard, ensuring she would be secure. Knowing my puppy, I seriously had my doubts about that, but Shelly signed off on final inspection.

While this construction was in progress, JD managed to lose four house keys in the course of two weeks on his way to and from school, causing Shelly to leave work for a rescue each time. I was proud when I returned home one night to participate in Shelly's decree that from now on, the last remaining house key was to reside on a snap shackle on Bebo's collar, out in her bungalow abode. She ordered that anyone wishing access to the home, would unlock the door and return the key to Bebo's collar before entering. It was the last key we ever had and it stayed latched to Bebo's collar for as long as I can remember. Shelly's rationale was that security was not to be considered because who, other than ourselves, would possibly attempt to procure this key from under the brilliant (often brushed by Shelly) white fangs of Bebo!

Bansai missed his puppy being outside and we took him out to visit Bebo every day. We would put Bansai on the sailboat shroud where he would survey the area, and eventually flap down to go see Bebo. We had to be observant because there were hawks, and neighboring cats to watch out for if Bansai was outside. Bebo enjoyed it when Bansai came to visit. She would roll around in the grass, careful not to touch the bird, until Bansai would ask her in some animal way to be still so he could climb up her front leg to come stand on her collar. It was an amazing interaction to watch.

ONE FOR
THE NEIGHBORS

One day at work I got a call from Shelly. She said, "Can you come home?"

"What's wrong?"

She said, "Come home," and hung up.

I advised my boss of this development and went dashing to my truck in the parking lot. As I raced home, I felt the acrid taste of anxiety rising on the back of my tongue, for I could only imagine what chess move my puppy had applied that eluded a solution from Shelly. I arrived at my home to find Shelly's best friend Lisa's car parked in the drive next to Shelly's car. I raced to the door noticing a sinister odor, but quickly dismissed it. When I entered the apartment, I found Lisa perched on our sofa reading one of my surf magazines. She did not look up, but I saw that exact same quirky smile that I observed Shelly deliver when I was wrestling the deer haunch from my puppy years ago. I heard quiet humming from the hallway and asked Lisa, "what's happening?" She dramatically swept her arm in the direction of the hallway, pointed, and didn't say a word.

As I approached our guest bathroom, the gentle humming continued as I stood in shock for a moment at the bathroom door. My bathroom looked like a scene from a B grade Halloween flick, with blood splotches all over the walls, counters, and floors. There were twenty to thirty empty two-liter V-8 bottles littering the counters and floor, helpfully delivered by Lisa. My beloved Shelly sat gracefully in the tub, twitching subtly with suppressed rage, humming gently to my puppy who's tail softly swished in the crimson Palm Beach Gardens spa. I could not help but notice how incredibly sexy my love's pert, petite breasts appeared, smeared with tomato juice, while she gently bathed my dog. Her beautiful blue-green eyes contrasting sharply with the bright red cocktail sauce.

Later, over beers and burgers across the street at my neighbors, I nervously listened to my neighbor's wife describe the short but disastrous debacle. Lisa had joined us and sat with me anticipating the story. My neighbor explained that she had stepped out onto the front porch with her infant daughter on her hip to investigate an unfamiliar neighborhood aroma. An instant later she watched my front door explode open with Shelly leaping out to screech, "WHAT are you doing!" as her eyes swept the front yard in search of my puppy. They both spotted Bebo at the same time, luxuriously rolling all over a quite beautiful, dead skunk under a scrub pine in the front yard. Where the dog procured the rodent, neither one of them knew.

Shelly launched into a sprint out the screen door across the front lawn, and Bebo instantly rolled to all-fours and snatched the putrid critter up by the scruff of the neck bounding to the defensive safety of the bunker between Shelly's car and the fence. My neighbor watched breathlessly as Shelly veered sharply to intercept my puppy but she was not fast enough. Shelly chased the dog around the car to bring them both to a dead end where the fence met the structure of the house. Shelly hurled a ladder leaning against the house in front of the car to come crashing down on top of the dog. She quickly put a foot heavily on the ladder pinning my now snarling puppy on the driveway, as she desperately yanked the not-long-deceased Pepé Le Pew from Bebo's snapping jaws. Bebo extricated herself from under the ladder while Shelly stood breathing hard with the dead skunk dangling by the tail from her hand. Shelly snatched the dog by the ear as she unceremoniously flung the dead animal to the curb. My neighbor said the loud yelps and howls of imagined pain issuing from my puppy were quite disturbing as Shelly dragged her by the ear to the screened patio. Shelly sat quietly through the entire oration offering no expansion of the details, Lisa was shaking her head through most of it, and I'm sure I was the only who noticed the subtle twitching once again.

Later, as we got ready for bed I made the mistake most young men do, opening my mouth before using my mind. I said to Shelly, "You still stink." As a result, Bebo and I spent the night rather uncomfortably in my hammock out front where I noticed she smelled, interestingly, of musk and Johnsons Baby Shampoo.

Of course, I had to explain my early departure from work to my boss the next day. As we sat in his office, he listened with a growing smile until laughing uncontrollably, then he promptly dismissed me. About fifteen minutes later, I was paged to the conference room. I arrived to find the senior staff all formally seated around the conference table. My boss invited me to take a seat and paused while I did so. Once seated, he then said, "Keith, I want you to explain to the organization why you left early yesterday."

Shortly thereafter, I got an unexpected, unexplained raise, and an invitation to lunch, encouraging me to invite my wife-to-be to accompany me.

NEW FRIENDS

One day, I was on the patio at my work station building a R/C model sailboat with Shelly working close by on her potted plants. My puppy was lazily dozing in the middle of the screened in patio.

Vince pulled in with his boss, Seth Carter, who gave Vince a ride home with his truck being in the shop. Seth was a stereotypical hillbilly from North Carolina, and sported a ZZ-Top beard that landed halfway down his chest. Not to allow looks to deceive you, Seth was very well off and owned the plumbing company, where Vince was apprenticing, with his two brothers. Seth was Vince's professional mentor and they were very good friends.

Vince must have invited Seth in for a beer or something, and as Vince and Seth walked up the drive approaching the screen door, Vince turned briefly to advise Seth, "Don't touch that dog." Shelly immediately echoed Vince's admonishment saying, "Don't touch that puppy." I heard my mind say "uh-oh," and began to turn away from my project to consider what I must do.

You must understand that circumstances in Bebo's life are decided instantly. She carefully reads the developing situation, immediately plans her course of action, and is perfectly content to negotiate the consequences of her actions when she is certain she has been successful. This entire process takes place in the amount of time it takes for your brain to perceive the image your optic nerve delivers when you open your eyelid. The dog is fantastically efficient at making decisions.

In one choreographed motion, I was completing my half-turn away from my work station as Vince and Seth stepped through the screen door onto the patio and Seth ignored the redundant warnings to lean forward toward Bebo saying, "Aaw, she ain't nothin but a little heel hound." As Seth's hand began to reach for the dog, Bebo launched off the floor to remove his jugular vein. Seth must have registered enough of the warning to expect this. As he instantly began to straighten, it left Bebo's lunge fractionally short and the dog clamped down on Seth's beard. My puppy began violently shaking Seth's face by the beard like a rag doll.

I was leaping to my feet to arrest my frenzied companion, but it was simply too late. My thoughts immediately took me back to the campground and the Canadian tourist, and what he must have experienced in my absence. Seth and Bebo, from the momentum of the attack, went summersaulting backward through the screen door, while Vince looked for an implement and Shelly quickly rearranged the garden hose.

As the snarling, screaming duo went rolling down the driveway, Seth must have managed to get a boot or a knee under Bebo because she went helicoptering across the front yard. My puppy instantly came charging back like a mad buffalo as Seth desperately attempted to climb into the back of his truck but did not make it. Bebo's jaws were latched on to Seth's boot preventing him from scrambling the rest of the way into the truck bed.

Shelly's bright green garden lariat appeared from nowhere to land over Bebo's back and the dog released the boot in stunned surprise, her head popping up to investigate, allowing the garden hose to flop around her torso. Shelly lurched on the hose at that instant, spinning my puppy away from Seth's dangerously compromised digit. I heard Seth issue from the back of the truck, "Holy shit!"

Bebo seemed to understand that Shelly had lassoed her for a reason. She came happily trotting to meet Shelly on the patio, lying under the garden hose backlash, to understand Shelly's greater meaning in this lesson. I was astoundingly impressed with Shelly's cow-punching skills, and referred her to Louis L'Amour's extensive writing on the subject. She did not seem to appreciate this referral.

UNTIL WE MEET AGAIN

It was not long after Bebo met her new friend Seth, that I lost her. One day I returned from work to bring Bebo out to relieve herself and enjoy the evening. Bebo seemed disoriented. She drunkenly relieved herself staggering around the yard. This of course immediately concerned me and I was glad when Shelly pulled up in the drive and joined me to inspect our daughter. I searched Bebo's limbs and muzzle for signs of a snake bite but found none. After our observation, we could only find mildly labored breathing, fevered looking eyes, and severely affected equilibrium to be the only symptoms of her affliction. We chose to observe Bebo for the evening unless her condition worsened, and take her to the vet in the morning unless her condition improved.

I had been with Shelly for almost seven years now, and Bebo was twelve years old. We did take Bebo to the vet the next morning and after some time and bloodwork, the doc advised us that she had contracted heartworms, and based on the larval count in her blood her condition was extreme. The doc went on to explain that Bebo would likely not survive the treatment of strychnine injections because of her age. He advised euthanizing her to save her from pain. Shelly and I were both shocked with instant grief. We could not choose that course of action at the time and chose to take Bebo home thinking perhaps she could enjoy a little more life with us enveloped with our love. It was very evident after only a couple days that this decision would be cruel, and we took her back to the doc to say good bye.

I was stricken with grief over the loss of my best friend, and returned to the surf to work through it in solitude. It was the first loss of a relationship holding the value of significant weight that I had ever experienced in my life. I spent weeks speaking to no one, and surfing constantly. After quite some time, I transitioned into acceptance and was grateful for Shelly's love and understanding through this period.

Bebo had taught me unmitigated devotion and unconditional love that I then practiced on Shelly with a newly inspired emphasis. God had indeed answered my plea for companionship in my life, with a twist. I sadly lost Shelly a few years ago as well, and I now find myself periodically chuckling as I think about what Jesus must be experiencing each day with my two girls. I can imagine him thinking it must be yet another test our Father is putting to him. I imagine a much different set of challenges for Jesus. In my hopes and prayers I envision, for example, my puppy accompanying Jonah on his fateful boat ride that day. I can see Shelly as the proud skipper of the vessel rescuing them from the divinely dispatched fish. I can imagine Jonah bouncing all his options off Bebo in the whale's belly, until the rhythmic thumping of her tail confirms he has come to the right one. I can see Shelly assisting the two relieved, wayward, messengers of God out of the blowhole, across the gang plank to her boat, then helpfully wiping whale goo off of them with the jib canvas.

I imagine the three of them taking a short reprieve of wine, goat cheese, and leavened bread, as Captain Shelly resumes the conversation, "…okay, what you want us to do now, boss? You want us to head over to Corinth and tell 'em they need to start paying attention?" I love both my girls with all my heart and soul, and I know they both reciprocated that love. I can imagine Jesus by his father's side, anxiously pleading, "…you can't be serious, how we gonna get 'em to revise the Bible down there! What do you reasonably expect me to do with these two?" Who could fail to have faith after witnessing God's greatest gift of love bestowed on both man and beast, with his grace.